SPECS

The True Story of Baseball Player George Toporcer

Thanks to Joseph Fetterman and Dan Bennett of the National Baseball Hall of Fame Library for their help with this book.

Copyright © 1990 American Teacher Publications
Published by Raintree Publishers Limited Partnership
All rights reserved. No part of this book may be reproduced or utilized in any form or by any means, electronic or mechanical, including photocopying, recording, or by any information storage and retrieval system without permission in writing from the Publisher. Inquiries should be addressed to Raintree Publishers, 310 West Wisconsin Avenue, Milwaukee, Wisconsin 53203.

Library of Congress number: 89-77943

Library of Congress Cataloging in Publication Data

Motomora, Mitchell.
  Specs: the true story of baseball player George Toporcer/ by Mitchell Motomora; illustrated by Nina Barbaresi.

  (Ready-set-read)
  Summary: A biography of baseball player George "Specs" Toporcer, who as a young boy was determined to play baseball at a time when few players wore glasses.
  1. Toporcer, George, 1899–1989—Juvenile literature. 2. Baseball players—United States—Biography—Juvenile literature. 3. St. Louis Cardinals (Baseball team)—History-Juvenile literature. [1. Toporcer, George. 1899–1989. 2. Baseball players.] I. Barbaresi, Nina, ill. II. Title. III. Title: True story of baseball player George Toporcer. IV. Series.
GV865.T63M68 1990 796.357'092—dc20
[B]
[92]   89-77943

ISBN 0-8172-3585-X

    2 3 4 5 6 7 8 9   94 93 92 91

READY•SET•READ

The True Story of Baseball Player
George Toporcer

by Mitchell Motomora
illustrated by Nina Barbaresi

Raintree Publishers
Milwaukee

This is the true story of a boy who loved to play baseball.

His real name was George, but everyone called him Specs. That's because he always wore spectacles, or glasses.

There was one problem. No one believed Specs could play ball. The coach wouldn't even let Specs try out for the school team.

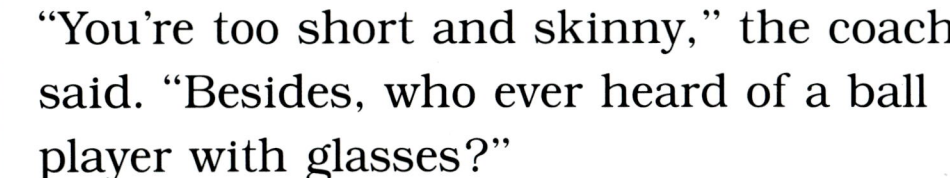
"You're too short and skinny," the coach said. "Besides, who ever heard of a ball player with glasses?"

Specs knew that it didn't matter what he looked like. What mattered was how he played. He started his own team.

When he played, everyone saw that. . .
WHAM! SLAM!
Specs was quite a ball player.

One day, Specs got a chance to play on his school team. Specs played well. Now the coach was glad to have Specs on his team.

When Specs grew up, he still loved baseball. He read everything he could about it.

Specs dreamed of playing for a major league team. He knew he had to keep practicing. After all, only the best players make it to the major leagues.

At last, Specs was asked to play for a team called the Cardinals. Specs had made it to the major leagues!

In 1926, the Cardinals had a chance to win the championship. All they had to do was beat the Giants.

The Giants were winning.

Then it was Specs's turn at bat. "Ha!" the pitcher thought. "This guy won't even see the ball!"
The pitcher was wrong.

WHAM! SLAM!
Specs got a hit! He helped his team win the game!
"Yeah! Specs! Hey, Specs!"

He was quite a ball player.

Sharing the Joy of Reading

Reading a book aloud to your child is just one way you can help your child experience the joy of reading. Now that you and your child have shared **Specs,** you can help your child begin to think and react as a reader by encouraging him or her to:

- Retell or reread the story with you, looking and listening for the repetition of specific letters, sounds, words, or phrases.

- Make a picture of a favorite character, event, or key concept from this book.

- Talk about his or her own ideas and feelings about the subject of this book and other things he or she might want to know about this subject.

Here is an activity that you can do together to help extend your child's appreciation of this book: You can help your child make his or her own personal baseball card. First, you and your child might want to look at a baseball card and discuss the kinds of information it contains. Then, take a piece of cardboard that is the size of a baseball card. On the front of the card, your child can place either a recent photograph or a self-portrait. On the back of the card, you can help your child list important information, including name, age, grade, height, weight, and favorite sport.